To Jay, Summer, Doody, Baci, and Nina-goose

NOTE FOR PARENTS:

This book introduces the Pretty Penny Saving Setup, a money-management tool easy enough for young children to understand. For each dollar Penny earns, she allots 10¢ for charitable causes, 20¢ for her long-term savings, and 70¢ for her everyday expenses. The 10%—20%—70% Saving Setup is a great way to begin shaping your child's saving and spending habits. As children grow, so will their money needs, so modify the Saving Setup as necessary over time. Happy saving!

Visit myprettypenny.com for fun activities and more.

Copyright © 2012 by Devon Kinch

All rights reserved. Published in the United States by
Random House Children's Books, a division of Random House, Inc., New York.
Random House and the colophon are registered trademarks
of Random House, Inc.

Visit us on the Web! www.randomhouse.com/kids

Educators and librarians, for a variety of teaching tools,
visit us at www.randomhouse.com/teachers

Visit Penny at myprettypenny.com

Library of Congress Cataloging-in-Publication Data
Kinch, Devon.
Pretty Penny cleans up / by Devon Kinch.
p. cm.
Audience: Ages 4–8.
Summary: In order to earn money for a concert, Pretty Penny and her friend Emma set up a puppy grooming salon.
ISBN 978-0-▓▓▓▓-6736-1 (trade) — ISBN 978-0-375-96736-8 (lib. bdg.)
1. Pet grooming salons—Juvenile fiction. 2. Dogs—Juvenile fiction. 3. Money-making projects for children—Juvenile fiction. [1. Pet grooming salons—Fiction. 2. Dogs—Fiction. 3. Moneymaking projects—Fiction.] I. Title.
PZ7.K5653Pc 2012 813.6—dc22 [E] 2010045882

MANUFACTURED IN CHINA
10 9 8 7 6 5 4 3 2 1
First Edition

Pretty Penny

Cleans Up

DEVON KINCH

RANDOM HOUSE 🏠 NEW YORK

It is the end of another busy day at the Small Mall. Penny and Iggy are pooped.

Penny's day started with a bakery bash—

and ended with a blowout book bonanza!

Penny is closing up shop when her best friend, Emma, stops by with her dog, Noodle.

The girls head outside to take Noodle for a walk.

Emma is upset. The Sassy Pants
concert is next week and she can't go.
 "I've spent all my allowance money, and
I can't afford a ticket," says Emma.
 "All of it?" asks Penny, surprised.
 "Every last cent," says Emma.

Emma needs five dollars for a ticket. That's a lot
of money! She doesn't know where she'll find it.
Penny wants to help Emma earn and save money.
She needs one of her big ideas . . . and fast!

So she starts to think. Emma thinks too.

The girls are stumped. Just when they both
get tired of thinking . . .

Voila! Penny gets her big idea! It was right there in
front of her.

"I know just what we'll do," explains Penny. "We're
going to open La Perfect Pup Salon for dogs. It'll be a hit!"

The next day Penny and Emma get to work setting
up La Perfect Pup Salon. The attic is full of goodies,
and it doesn't take long for Iggy to find a box of wacky
wigs. Noodle stumbles upon a box of beautiful bows.
Penny discovers the most perfect barber chair, and Emma
arrives with a basket of colorful ribbons and a few of her
favorite barrettes to share. Grandma Bunny helps the girls
get organized.

The girls practice their styles on Iggy and Noodle.

They are clearly experts.

They have everything they need to open up shop.
"But wait!" exclaims Penny. "We forgot something!"

"Take a look at this. This is the
PRETTY PENNY SAVING SETUP.
I use it each time I earn money. Here's
how it works:

"FIRST, you need a box.
This box is for saving money
for the future. You lock it
with this key.

"SECOND, you need a jar. This jar is for sharing money—or for giving money to charity. Someone may need this money more than you.

"THIRD, you need a purse. This purse is for money that you can spend—like for Sassy Pants tickets!"

It's the grand opening of the salon, and the girls are
ready to get started. Penny and Emma greet their very first
customer.

"Hi, Piper," says Emma. "Welcome to La Perfect Pup
Salon."

"Please give my pup, Barker, the Modern do," says Piper.

"I'd like the Punk
for my little Buttercup,"
says Maggie.

"Goose and Chunk
will have the Regal,"
says Buck.

Bunny and her friend
Trish stop by the salon
with their pets.
"Bo and Nugget will
have the Classic do,
please," says Bunny.

Before they know it, the girls have
five dogs and one cat to pamper.

Penny and Emma get right to work. But Chunk can't
sit still! Barker won't stop barking! Noodle loves the
bubbles! Buttercup is a perfect angel, while Goose falls in
love at first sight.

Splish! Splash! Bark! Crash! Wet dogs are everywhere!
What a mess!

Penny is in a panic. They have so much work to do.
How are they ever going to manage?

Iggy to the rescue!

Iggy gets busy cleaning up, Emma does the combing and brushing, and Penny is in charge of braiding and weaving beautiful ribbons into each dog's fur.

Soon each pet is perfect. Bo looks beautiful. Penny and Emma finish just in time, and the salon is sparkling clean!

Everyone returns to pick up the pampered pets.

"Barker looks just darling," says Piper. "How much do I owe you?"

"That will be five dollars," replies Emma.

"Thank you very much!" says Penny.

le Perfect Pup Salon

SHOP:

NAME	PUPPY	DO
Maggie	Buttercup	The Punk
Bunny	Bo (the cat)	The Classic
Trish	Nugget	The Classic
Piper	Barker	The Modern
Buck	Goose & Chunk	The Regal
Emma	Noodle	The Punk

The Official
Small Mall Ledger

STYLIST	PRICE
	$5.00
	$5.00
Emma	$5.00
Emma	$5.00
Penny	$10.00
Penny	$5.00 FREE
Penny & Emma	
Emma	
GRAND TOTAL:	$30.0

Now that their work is done, Penny opens the register and starts counting their earnings.

They worked very hard and made thirty dollars! Penny divides the money evenly.

"That's fifteen dollars for you and fifteen dollars for me," explains Penny.

"We did it!" Emma cheers. "We made a fortune!"

"Not so fast," says Penny. "You need to use the Saving Setup."

The girls find a safe place for the
Saving Setup in Emma's room.

"We earned enough money to save for the
future, give to charity, and spend on Sassy
Pants tickets!" explains Penny.

Emma places three dollars in her savings
box. She locks it with her key.

She sets aside
another one dollar
and fifty cents for her
sharing jar.

Then she puts ten dollars
and fifty cents in her spending
purse.

Emma is proud. "Saving
money is so much fun," she says.

Today is the Sassy Pants concert. Penny and Emma are very excited that La Perfect Pup Salon was such a success. Now they each can afford to buy a ticket with their spending money!

"We really cleaned up!" says Penny.

"Yeah! La Perfect Pup Salon rocks!" says Emma.